SCOOP

CBeebies
BBC

Hi, I'm Scoop.

I'm a yellow digger. I have a big front scoop for shovelling sand and gravel, and a back scoop for digging holes.

One day Bob and Wendy were busy, so they left me in charge. It wasn't as easy as I'd thought it would be…

Bob and Wendy had to go to an important lunch at the town hall.

"What about finishing off the Mayor's new garage?" I asked.

"You'll have to be in charge today, Scoop," said Bob.

I felt really proud.

"Can I fix it? Yes, I can!" I said.

I took Muck and Lofty to the Mayor's garage. I felt very important when I told them about the job we had to do.

"Oooh, watch out, Scoop's in charge!" teased Muck.

"Stop being silly, you two. Let's get started!" I said.

"Right, Muck, you pass the roofing section to Lofty and he can lift it onto the roof," I told the others. "Quickly, now. We haven't got all day!"

"Huh, aren't you going to help, Scoop?" grumbled Muck.

"I am helping. I'm in charge!"
I said crossly.

"Oooh, Scoop's in charge!" giggled
Muck and Lofty.

"Come on, let's get on with the work,"
I shouted. "I want Bob and Wendy to
be proud of us, that's all!"

Being in charge was hard work!

We were busy working when Mr Bentley, the building inspector, came to check the Mayor's garage.

"Where's Bob?" he asked.

"He's gone to lunch at the town hall," said Muck.

"I'm in charge today," I said proudly.

"Yes, Scoop's in charge!" giggled Muck and Lofty, again.

Mr Bentley took his coat off to inspect the new garage.

"I don't want to scratch my watch, so I'd better take that off, too," he said, as he put it on top of his coat. I moved forwards to show him the work we had done.

"**Stop, Scoop!**" he yelled. **Scrunch!** Oh no! My tyres crunched over his watch.

At the town hall, the Mayor had presented Bob with a special watch for all the hard work he'd done that year.

"Let's go and show the team," said Bob excitedly.

"Oh, yes!" said Wendy. "They'll be so proud of you."

"What a good job you've made of the garage, Scoop," said Bob, when he and Wendy arrived back.

"I haven't really," I said. "I was showing off and being bossy and now I've smashed Mr Bentley's watch."

"Don't worry," said Bob. "Mr Bentley, you can have my new watch."

Mr Bentley was delighted.

Back at the yard I felt very miserable.

"What's the matter, Scoop?" asked Wendy. "You look sad."

"I feel terrible. I got too big for my boots and bossed everybody around!" I cried.

"I'm sure you weren't that bad," said Wendy, kindly.

Just then, Mr Bentley arrived at the yard.

"The Mayor is so pleased with his new garage, he asked me to give you this!" Mr Bentley said as he handed Bob another new watch.

"I think Scoop should have it," said Bob. "He was in charge."

"I don't deserve it!" I said.

"Oh, you weren't that bad!" said Lofty.

"You have it Bob, I don't know where I'd wear it." I said.

"Good old Scoop!" Bob laughed.

THE END!